SAN BERNARDINO PUBLIC LIBRARY

W9-AUB-582

SAN BERNARDINO PUBLIC LIBRARY
3 9876 00143 3513

J917.3 FLE   central

WITHDRAWN

Fleming, Alice M. $13.00

The king of Prussia and a
  peanut butter sandwich 1988

③ ——

CHILDREN'S ROOM

**SAN BERNARDINO
PUBLIC LIBRARY**

San Bernardino, California

A fine will be charged on books and
other materials kept overtime. Careful use
of materials is expected and any soiling,
damage or loss must be paid for by the bor-
rower.

The King of Prussia
and a
Peanut Butter Sandwich

ALICE FLEMING

The King of Prussia
and a

Peanut Butter Sandwich

Illustrated by
RONALD HIMLER

CHARLES SCRIBNER'S SONS • NEW YORK

The publishers gratefully acknowledge the kind assistance
of Mr. John D. Thiesen, Acting Director of the
Mennonite Library and Archives, North Newton, Kansas.

Text copyright © 1988 by Alice Fleming
Illustrations copyright © 1988 by Ronald Himler

All rights reserved. No part of this book may be reproduced or transmitted in any
form or by any means, electronic or mechanical, including photocopying, record-
ing, or by any information storage and retrieval system, without permission in
writing from the Publisher.

Charles Scribner's Sons Books for Young Readers
Macmillan Publishing Company · 866 Third Avenue, New York, NY 10022
Collier Macmillan Canada, Inc.

Printed in the United States of America
First Edition   10 9 8 7 6 5 4 3 2 1

11/7/8
$13.00
Centra
J917.3
FLE

Library of Congress Cataloging-in-Publication Data
Fleming, Alice Mulcahey, 1928–
The king of Prussia and a peanut butter sandwich.
Summary: Narrates the saga of how the Mennonites left Prussia to avoid military
service, went to southern Russia where they learned to raise Turkey Red wheat,
and ultimately came to the United States where they helped make Kansas famous
for its wheat.
  1. Mennonites—United States—History—19th Century—Juvenile literature. 2. Russian Germans—United States—History—19th century—Juvenile
literature. 3. Mennonites—History—Juvenile literature. 4. Russian Germans—History—Juvenile literature. 5. Turkey red wheat—Kansas—Newton
Region—History—19th century—Juvenile literature. 6. Newton Region
(Kan.)—History—Juvenile literature.
[1. Mennonites—History. 2. Turkey red wheat. 3. Wheat. 4. Newton Region (Kan.)—History. 5. United States—History—1865–1898] I. Himler,
Ronald, ill. II. Title.
E184.M45F58 1988 973′.088287   87-9718   ISBN 0-684-18880-5

The King of Prussia
and a
Peanut Butter Sandwich

Is there any connection between the King of Prussia and a peanut butter sandwich? That sounds like a joke or a riddle, but it's really the beginning of a true story.

The story starts in Prussia—a kingdom in what is now East Germany—long before peanut butter sandwiches were invented. It involves a king, an empress, a czar, a President of the United States, and a group of boys and girls.

The king's name was Frederick the Great. He ruled Prussia from 1740 to 1786. Frederick became "the Great" by fighting wars with most of his neighbors in Europe. He gobbled up their lands and turned Prussia into a large and powerful nation.

After he had created a large and powerful nation, Frederick needed a large and powerful army to defend it. That was no problem for the king. All he had to do was issue an order: *From now on every able-bodied man in Prussia will be required to report for military service.*

Most of the able-bodied men in Prussia obeyed the king's order. They wouldn't dare do anything else. But there were some men who were not going to obey, no matter what. They belonged to the Mennonite Church, and the Mennonites didn't believe in joining armies or fighting wars.

What were they going to do? The leaders of each of the Mennonite villages in Prussia got together to decide. They scratched their heads and tugged their beards and cleared their throats. In the end, they decided there was only one thing they *could* do: leave Prussia and move someplace where all the able-bodied men would not have to report for military service.

The next question was: where? It had to be someplace where they could attend their own churches and schools. And someplace where there was plenty of room to farm. If there was anything the Mennonites loved, next to God and their families, it was making things grow.

In some of the communities, the leaders recommended a move across the ocean. The people in those villages packed their belongings and sailed to America. They settled in the state of Pennsylvania, and because they came from Prussia, which was part of *Deutschland,* or Germany, they became known as the Pennsylvania Dutch.

In other Mennonite communities, the leaders recommended a move in the opposite direction. The people in their villages loaded their clothes and kettles and chests and chairs and shovels and sickles and spades into their farm wagons. Then they hitched up their horses and set out, several dozen families at a time, in long wagon trains.

They traveled east through Poland and south through Russia, lurching along in their wagons, day after day, week after week, until they came to the southernmost

shore of the Russian province of Ukraine.

"Are we there yet?" the Mennonite children demanded for the eighty-eighth time.

"Not yet," their parents replied wearily.

The wagon trains wended their way along the coast of the Black Sea until they came to a narrow strip of land.

"Are we there yet?" the Mennonite children demanded for the eighty-ninth time.

"Not yet," their parents said. "But it won't be too much longer."

And it wasn't. The wagon trains lumbered across the narrow strip of land, and after a few miles the drivers reined in their horses.

"Now we're here," the Mennonite parents announced, and everyone—mothers and fathers and children, grand-mothers, grandfathers, brothers, sisters, uncles, aunts, cousins, even the dogs and cats—tumbled out of their wagons to see what "here" looked like.

The narrow strip of land the Mennonites had just crossed runs between the Black Sea and a much smaller body of water called the Sea of Azov. It forms a bridge between the Ukraine and the Crimean Peninsula.

The peninsula—a large chunk of land shaped like a piece from a jigsaw puzzle—was the Mennonites' new home. They had decided to settle there because Catherine the Great, Empress of all the Russias, had made them an unbelievable offer.

As soon as she heard they were planning to leave Prussia, the empress sent them a message: "Come and settle in Crimea. I'll give you all the land you need to start new farms. I'll let you worship in your own churches and send your children to your own schools. And I'll grant you a one-hundred-year exemption from serving in the Russian Army."

Why was Catherine so good to the Mennonites? It certainly wasn't because she shared their dislike of war. On the contrary, her armies were on the march as often as King Frederick's.

No, Catherine had another reason for being good to the Mennonites. She had recently seized the Crimean Peninsula from Turkey, and she was hoping these hard-working Prussians could transform its grassy treeless plains—the Russians call them steppes—into an area of thriving farms.

Catherine was so anxious to have the Mennonites settle in Crimea that one of the other things she promised them was the right to continue speaking their native German.

Before long, Crimea looked like a corner of Prussia. The villages had Prussian names, like Halbstadt, Rosenort, and Tiegenhagen, and they were built in the Prussian style—the houses lined up side by side along a single wide street, with their gable ends facing the front.

The houses stood on tiny plots of land. There was just enough room to plant a few flowers in the front yard and a few vegetables in the back. The real farming was done on much larger tracts—175 acres to a family—that began on the edge of town.

The most important thing the Mennonites had to decide was what to raise on their 175 acres. Although the soil in Crimea was rich, there wasn't much rainfall. They would have to find crops that could survive in a dry climate. In the meantime, since there was no shortage of grass, they decided to raise sheep.

One of the first things the Mennonites discovered about sheep-farming in Crimea was that it could be a very dangerous occupation. The land had belonged to Turkey for so many years that a group of roving Turkish tribesmen called Tartars refused to believe it no longer did. They ignored Catherine the Great's orders not to trespass on Mennonite land and continued to come galloping across the steppes whenever they pleased.

The savage Tartars regularly swooped down on the newcomers' pastures. They tore through their fences, scattered their herds, and ran their deadly steel-tipped pikes through anyone who got in their way.

The Mennonites learned to be on the lookout for Tartars. They waved them off with pitchforks and scythes and respectfully reminded the Empress of all the Russias that she had ordered the tribesmen not to trespass on Mennonite land.

Nobody knows for certain, but it seems likely that Catherine the Great—who didn't like Tartars in the first place and had a ferocious temper in the second—flew into a rage. This time she sent soldiers to patrol the frontier between Russia and Turkey, and the Tartars stopped their raids.

The Mennonites experimented with all sorts of crops—flax and tobacco and melons, potatoes and cabbage and beans. Most of them withered and died from lack of rainfall.

Then some clever Mennonite farmer had an idea. Why not cultivate half your land one year and the other half the next? The land that wasn't cultivated might retain the year's rainfall and provide enough moisture for the crops that were planted the following year.

Once they discovered dry farming, as this system is called, the Mennonites thought they could raise whatever they pleased. It didn't take them long to find out they couldn't.

The crops that used to wither and die from lack of rainfall now lived long enough to develop plant diseases. There were several different types, and almost all of them were as contagious as the sniffles and far more serious. They often killed an entire year's crop.

Insects were another menace. Many a farmer had to stand helplessly by while the onions or potatoes he had so carefully planted and tended were completely devoured by one or another of the various bugs that came buzzing across the steppes as soon as the weather got hot.

The Mennonites were discouraged. Who wouldn't be? They had outwitted Crimea's droughts only to be defeated by its blights and bugs. Surely there must be something that would grow on these fertile plains. If only they could find out what!

There were some Turkish farmers who had been living in Crimea when the Mennonites arrived. Their farms were small and scraggly and not very well kept, but their crops never seemed to fail.

The Mennonites found it hard to believe that these lazy Turks knew something about farming that they didn't.

"What's their secret?" the Mennonites wondered. They began studying the Turks' farming habits and discovered that they were raising wheat. Not just any old wheat, but a special kind called winter wheat.

Instead of being planted in the spring so it could grow during the summer and be harvested in the fall, winter wheat was planted in the fall so it could grow during the winter and be harvested in the spring.

By the time summer rolled around and the crops were threatened by droughts and blights and bugs, the Turkish farmers didn't have to worry. Their winter wheat had long since been harvested and sent to market.

"It looks as if these Turks know more about farming than we thought," the Mennonites were forced to admit. "Perhaps we should try planting winter wheat."

The Mennonites were not the kind of farmers who simply tossed their seeds into the ground and hoped for the best. They were always looking for ways to improve their

crops. They had no sooner coaxed their first batch of winter wheat seeds into taking root and growing than they started thinking of ways to make the wheat grow better.

Several of the Mennonites were experts at plant breeding. They took the original seeds and bred them into a new and extremely hardy variety of wheat called Turkey Red (for the Turks who first planted it and for the color of its seeds).

Turkey Red wheat quickly became the Mennonites'— and Russia's—most important crop. It was a hard wheat, the kind that is ground into flour for making bread. (Soft wheat is used for making pastries and dumplings.) In Russia, and everywhere else in Europe, bread was served at every meal. In poorer families, bread *was* the meal.

In a few years, Crimea was dotted with prosperous farms and bustling villages. In a few more years, the Mennonite settlements had multiplied at such a rate that they spread beyond the Crimean Peninsula and into southern Ukraine.

A city called Berdyansk grew up along the Sea of Azov. Its principal industries were milling flour and shipping grain. The ships that left the docks at Berdyansk sailed through the Sea of Azov to the Black Sea and on into the Mediterranean Sea, carrying Turkey Red wheat to ports all over the world.

Time passed and the children who had asked, "Are we there yet?" grew up and had children of their own. They got older and older and eventually died. More time passed and their children and grandchildren did the same thing.

The decades came and went faster than anyone could have imagined until one day the Mennonites looked at the calendar and realized that their one-hundred-year exemption from serving in the Russian army was almost up.

The leaders of each of the Mennonite villages in southern Russia got together to decide what to do. They scratched their heads and tugged their beards and cleared their throats just as the leaders in Prussia had done a hundred years before.

Catherine the Great was dead and Russia had a new ruler, Czar Alexander II. The czar seemed like a fair-minded man. Perhaps if they asked him politely, he would agree to extend the Mennonites' exemption.

As it turned out, the czar was a fair-minded man. Unfortunately, he was so fair-minded that he couldn't bring himself to excuse the Mennonites from military service when everyone else was being drafted.

The leaders of the Mennonite communities had another idea. A group of them made an appointment to see the United States consul in Berdyansk. He was stationed there to look after American interests in the area.

"How can I help you?" he asked the solemn, bearded farmers who crowded into his office.

The Mennonites wasted no time in telling him.

"Would it be possible for our people to emigrate to the United States?" they asked.

"Yes," said the consul, "I think it would."

Back in the 1870s, the United States was a surprisingly uncrowded country. The flag that flew outside the U.S. consul's office had thirteen stripes but only thirty-five stars. Several of the states those thirty-five stars represented were begging for settlers.

"There are huge tracts of land in Minnesota, Kansas, and Nebraska," the consul told his visitors. "Most of it is owned by the railroads that are starting to crisscross the

country, but they'll sell it for practically nothing to anyone who wants to live there."

Why would the railroads do that, the Mennonites
wondered.

"Because," the consul explained, "once the land has
settlers, the railroads will make money carrying pas-
sengers and freight."

The Mennonites thought they might be interested in
buying some of these railroad lands.

"All right," said the consul. "I'll start making the ar-
rangements."

Before long, a steamship arrived in Berdyansk, and a passenger named C.B. Schmidt strode down the gangplank. Mr. Schmidt was an agent for the Santa Fe Railroad. He spent most of his time traveling around Europe talking to people who might want to emigrate to the United States and settle along the Santa Fe's lines.

The Mennonites liked Mr. Schmidt for several reasons. He had originally come from Germany, so they could talk to him in their own language. On top of that, he was as honest and plain-spoken as they were.

"The Santa Fe recently extended its line to a town called Newton, Kansas," he said. "There's plenty of good farmland out there, but I wouldn't expect you to buy it sight unseen. Why don't you send a few of your people over to take a look at it?"

The Mennonites thought that sounded like good advice. A few weeks later a dozen German-speaking farmers from as many villages in southern Russia made the long voyage through the Sea of Azov to the Black Sea, through the Black Sea to the Mediterranean Sea, through the Mediterranean Sea to the Atlantic Ocean, and across the Atlantic Ocean to the United States.

The Mennonites had barely stepped off the boat when they stepped onto a train that would take them more than a thousand miles across the country to Kansas. As they chugged westward, they passed through fewer and fewer big cities. The hills and valleys they had seen from the train window when they started out disappeared, and the landscape flattened out to become one enormous plain.

The train rattled across the Missouri River into Kansas and headed west toward Newton. If the Mennonites had been city people instead of farmers, they might have been upset to see that Kansas was nothing but wide open spaces. Since they were farmers, they couldn't have been happier. More land meant more room to farm.

Mr. Schmidt took his visitors on a tour of Newton and introduced them to some of the farmers who had already settled there. The Mennonites asked all sorts of questions about the soil and the climate and the annual rainfall. They looked and listened and nodded their heads.

Then they turned to Mr. Schmidt with the most important question of all: Would the President of the United States expect them to serve in the army?

"I don't know," said Mr. Schmidt. "But if you really want to find out, why don't you go home by way of Washington, D.C., and ask the president in person?"

Mr. Schmidt wasn't kidding. In those days, presidents weren't as busy as they are now so they had more time for visitors.

The president at that time was Ulysses S. Grant, the country's most famous soldier. Grant had graduated from the United States Military Academy at West Point and had been the commanding general of the Union Army during the Civil War. He and the Mennonites couldn't have been farther apart on the subject of soldiering, but that didn't stop them from having a cordial visit.

The president told the Mennonites he hoped they'd settle in Kansas. The Mennonites said they'd like to but only on one condition. They didn't believe in joining armies or fighting wars. Would the president promise them that if they came to the United States, they wouldn't have to do either one?

President Grant shook his head.

"I'm afraid I can't do that," he said.

The Mennonites were baffled. They were used to living in a country where the rulers could do whatever they pleased.

"Things are different here in the United States," the president said. "The people elect representatives to Congress, and Congress makes most of the decisions, including who will and will not serve in the army."

Then perhaps the Mennonites should talk to Congress about an exemption?

"I don't think that's necessary," the president said. "The United States has been in existence for almost a hundred years. It's already fought several wars. And in all that time, Congress has never forced anyone to serve in the army if it violated his religious beliefs."

The Mennonites found that hard to believe.

"It's true," Grant assured them. "And I give you my word that it always will be. Religious freedom is one of the basic principles of our government."

It was a long trip back across the Atlantic Ocean, through the Mediterranean Sea to the Black Sea, through the Black Sea to the Sea of Azov, and across the Sea of Azov to Berdyansk. The leaders of the Mennonite communities had plenty of time to think about what President Grant had told them.

By the time their ship docked in Berdyansk, their minds were made up. They returned to their villages and told their people that the area around Newton, Kansas, would be their new home.

And what was the area around Newton, Kansas, like, the people wanted to know.

"The soil and climate are almost identical to Crimea's," their leaders reported. "It looks like a perfect place to grow Turkey Red wheat."

And what about serving in the army?

"We met with the President of the United States himself," the leaders replied. "He says that in his country people don't have to serve in the army if it violates their religious beliefs."

The Mennonites offered prayers of thanksgiving for President Grant, the United States of America, the Santa Fe Railroad, and Mr. C. B. Schmidt. Then they set about planning their departure from Russia.

The best time to go, they agreed, would be summer. They could harvest their last crop of Russian wheat that spring, spend the summer traveling and getting settled, and plant their first crop of American wheat the following fall.

The Mennonites made their travel plans as carefully as they did everything else. There wasn't much room for baggage on a steamship, so one of the most important things they had to do was sort through their belongings and decide what to bring.

The first item on every family's list was the Bible. The second was a sack full of Turkey Red wheat seeds. They couldn't be just any old wheat seeds, however. They had to be hardy enough to survive and thrive in the untried soil of Kansas. Only the most perfect seeds would do.

Mennonite families may have been more religious and more hard-working than other families, but when it came to assigning jobs, they were very much the same. The most important ones went to the grownups. The second most important ones went to the older brothers and sisters, and the ones that everyone else was too big or too busy to do went to—who else?—the younger brothers and sisters.

This time, things were different. In Mennonite families all over southern Russia, the younger brothers and sisters were finally given an important job.

The week before they were scheduled to sail to America, all the boys and girls over the age of six or seven and under the age of ten or eleven were summoned to the barns where the newly harvested wheat was stored. Their fathers would scoop up a handful of grain and sift carefully through the kernels until they spotted one that was a rich deep red and hard as a small stone.

"See," they would say, holding it out to the boys and girls. "This is the kind of perfect seed you must select for us."

The boys and girls in each family were given brown
burlap bushel bags. "When the bag is full, your job will
be done," their fathers told them.

Filling those brown burlap bushel bags turned out to
be a lot harder than the boys and girls had expected.
There were very few seeds that were the perfect shade of
red or the perfect degree of hardness. Sometimes several
dozen handfuls of grain were scooped up and scrutinized
and not a single good seed turned up.

Some of the boys and girls didn't have much patience. Midway through the first morning, they became cranky and marched off to complain to their mothers. They were hot. They were tired. They were thirsty. Their heads hurt. They didn't want to collect seeds anymore.

Their mothers gave them slices of strudel and mugs of milk and shooed them back to the barns. Midway through the first afternoon, the same thing happened.

Only this time some of their older brothers and sisters heard them complaining.

"Stop acting like babies," they scolded.

"We're not acting like babies," the boys and girls replied.

"Yes, you are!"

"No, we're not!"

"Yes, you are!"

By the middle of the second day some of the boys and girls had a layer of seeds on the bottom of their brown burlap bushel bags, but it was going to take at least a thousand of those layers to reach the top.

"Maybe we don't have to reach the top," somebody suggested. "Maybe halfway will do."

Halfway wouldn't do.

"The bags have to be filled to the top," the Mennonite mothers and fathers insisted.

"But it's going to take *forever*," the boys and girls wailed.

"No, it's not," their mothers and fathers said firmly. "Just keep on working, and before you know it the bags will be full."

The boys and girls didn't believe them, but they knew better than to say so. There was something about the looks on their mothers' and fathers' faces that told them that it didn't matter if they were hot, and tired, and

thirsty, and their heads hurt, and they didn't want to collect seeds anymore. They had to do it just the same.

A few of the boys and girls got sulky. A few got the slows. But most of them got smart. If they couldn't get out of working, they decided, they might as well try to make the job less boring.

Singing songs helped. So did telling stories. Counting the seeds was even better. Once you reached a hundred, it only took half as long to reach two hundred. Then before you knew it, you had reached five hundred, then a thousand, then two thousand, then five thousand.

The work went faster. The grumbling died down. And the brown burlap bushel bags stopped looking droopy and forlorn and began to stand up straight and puff out their sides. By the end of the week, one of the girls let out a whoop of triumph. She had counted 850,000 wheat seeds and her brown burlap bushel bag was completely full.

A few seconds later one of the boys let out a whoop. Then one of the girls. Then one of the boys again. The whoops came faster and faster. The job was over. Every one of the brown burlap bushel bags was finally full.

"See," said the boys' and girls' parents. "That wasn't so bad, was it?"

The boys and girls shook their heads. Now that it was over, it really wasn't.

The Mennonites left Russia one village at a time. All the families booked passage on the same ship so they could arrive in Kansas at the same time and start building their new villages together.

The first group of families arrived in Newton, Kansas, in the summer of 1873. They stumbled off the train lugging trunks and valises and carefully clutching their brown burlap bushel bags full of seeds.

The weather was hot and dry just as it was in southern Russia.

"Good weather for raising corn," the other farmers in Newton told their new neighbors. "Too bad you didn't get here early enough to plant some."

The Mennonites nodded politely and turned their attention to sectioning off their land and digging the foundations for their homes.

By fall, the area around Newton was dotted with brand new farmhouses, and the Mennonites were ready to untie their brown burlap bushel bags and start planting winter wheat.

The other farmers in Newton shook their heads. These Mennonites must be crazy. Why were they planting in

the fall when everyone else planted in the spring? And why were they planting wheat when everyone else planted corn?

Well, it was the Mennonites' business, not theirs, the other farmers shrugged. If that's the way they wanted to do things, let them.

The Mennonites didn't know what the other farmers were saying about them. Even if they'd known, they wouldn't have cared. The only question on their minds was: would their Turkey Red wheat grow as well on the Great Plains of Kansas as it had on the steppes of Russia? They wouldn't know the answer until they saw their first crop.

The Mennonites spent most of the winter worrying. Even the boys and girls—who didn't usually worry—worried. After all their hard work collecting the seeds, wouldn't it be awful if none of them grew?

When the spring of 1874 arrived, everyone stopped worrying. The Turkey Red seeds that the boys and girls had so carefully selected came up strong and tall and healthy. The Mennonites thanked God and patted their children on their heads. Kansas was a good place to be.

The other farmers watched the new immigrants harvesting their wheat in early June and shook their heads once more.

"What's wrong with these Mennonites?" they asked each other. "They plant when everyone else is harvesting and harvest when everyone else is planting."

Before long, the other farmers stopped fretting about the Mennonites. They had other problems on their minds.

The summer of 1874 was even hotter and drier than the summer of 1873. As the weeks passed, the dry spell turned into a full-scale drought. By the Fourth of July, every farmer in Kansas was anxiously scanning the sky for rain clouds.

July slipped into August and not a single dark cloud appeared. Then one afternoon the sky suddenly turned black. The birds stopped chirping, and the chickens, thinking night had fallen, scurried to their roosts. An instant later there was a weird whirring sound, and something that felt like hailstones dropped out of the sky.

Within minutes, the huge black cloud lifted and the sun reappeared. Everyone could see that what had felt like hailstones was something stranger and much, much scarier—grasshoppers.

There were millions of them, all tangled together in crawling, gnawing, awful clumps. They carpeted the

ground and clung to people's clothes. They landed on the trees in swarms so thick they sent the branches crashing to the ground. They devoured the leaves, the grass, and the corn, and when they had finished eating the crops, they gnawed on the handles of rakes and hoes and ate the horses' harnesses.

There was barely a square inch of Kansas that wasn't covered with grasshoppers. In some places they clustered along the railroad tracks in layers thick enough to stop the most powerful locomotives.

The disaster left everyone in Kansas in a state of shock. First they and their families had been frightened almost to death. Then before they knew what was happening, their entire year's crop—and the money they hoped to make from it—had been eaten away by insects.

The only farmers who weren't ruined by the rain of grasshoppers were the Mennonites. Their practice of planting in the fall and harvesting in the spring had saved them.

The summer of 1874 was a sad time in Kansas. Some of the farmers were so discouraged that they abandoned their land and left the state. The rest were determined to hold on to their farms and struggle along until they could harvest another year's crop.

Two things happened that made their struggle easier. The first was that the rest of the country read about the

disaster in the newspapers and rushed to send donations of food, clothes, and money to help the troubled Kansans. The second was that the Mennonites offered to give as many Turkey Red wheat seeds as they could spare to anyone who wanted them.

That fall half the farmers in Kansas were planting instead of harvesting. By spring, they were doing precisely the opposite. Hard winter wheat turned out to be such a good crop—and Turkey Red such a good type—that within a few years every farmer in the state was rushing to buy seeds.

Before long, the Great Plains of Kansas were as famous for their wheat as the vast steppes of Russia. They still are.

A large share of the flour that is produced in the United States each year comes from Kansas wheat. A large share of that flour is used in baking bread. And a large share of that bread is used in making peanut butter sandwiches.

Perhaps you'll think of the Mennonites the next time you have one. You may also think of the King of Prussia who started it all. And while you're at it, don't forget Catherine the Great, Czar Alexander II, President Grant, and—most important of all—the boys and girls who collected the Turkey Red seeds.

AUTHOR'S NOTE

My interest in the Mennonites and Turkey Red wheat began when I happened upon the subject in *The Concise Dictionary of American History*. The entry was only a few paragraphs long, but it noted that the Mennonite children had collected the seeds that were brought from Crimea to Kansas and mentioned one of those children, an eight-year-old named Anna Barkman, who remembered as an old woman what a tedious job it had been.

That brief entry was enough to send me racing to the library to find out more. As I soon discovered, there is scarcely a history of the Mennonites, of Kansas, or of American agriculture that does not contribute to the story. Among the many books I consulted, the most helpful were C. Henry Smith's *The Story of the Mennonites,* which offers a wealth of information about the exodus from Prussia, the resettlement in Crimea, and the eventual move to America, and Kenneth S. Davis's *Kansas, A Bicentennial History,* which includes vivid descriptions of the grasshopper invasion and shows the crucial role the Mennonites played in the economic development of Kansas.

To the best of my knowledge, the historical facts in this book are accurate. It should be pointed out, however, that there were—and still are—many communities of Mennonites. Not all of them left Russia at the same time, nor did they all emigrate to Kansas. Some went to other states, such as Minnesota and the Dakotas, and another group settled in Canada.

INDEX